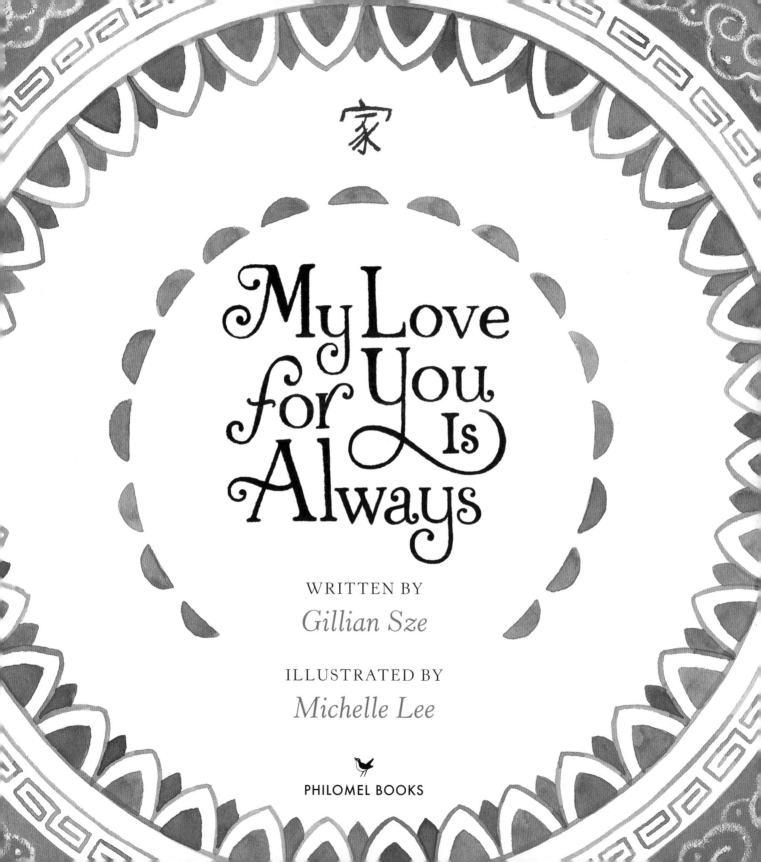

家

My Love for You, Is Always

WRITTEN BY

Gillian Sze

ILLUSTRATED BY

Michelle Lee

PHILOMEL BOOKS

Mama, do you love me?

Yes, my child, of course I do.

But what is love, Mama?

Hm . . . Love is many things at once.

And it is different for every person,

so it can be hard to describe.

Ah . . . but if I touched love, what would it feel like?

Let's see . . . Well, my love for you feels warm.

Like tea in my tummy.

What does it smell like?

Like all of my favorite spices.

My love for you is as fragrant as star anise,

as rich as cardamom and cloves.

Mama, what does love look like?

It's painted in my favorite color, my child.
Rosy as wolfberries and bright as persimmons.

But Mama,
I don't like persimmons.

Then how about oranges?

My love is as bright as orange zest.

It glows like bamboo leaves in the afternoon.

Does it make a sound?

Yes, I think so.

Sometimes it's crisp like winter radish.

Other times it's quiet like simmering broth.

What does love taste like, Mama?

Mmm, it tastes sweeter than the red dates I put in your soup.

My love is that savored first bite of spun sugar.

How does love move?

It darts from rivers to oceans.

Sometimes my love swims

in circles like a carp.

It shines through the water

like its own brilliant sun.

*Mama, how **much** do you love me?*

I love you more than all the grains of rice

in all the fields in the world, my child.

That's a lot, right?

More than you know.

Can you tell this to me again, Mama?

Yes, and many times more. Again and again.

Why?

Because my love for you is always.

It goes round and round like the gold rim of your bowl . . .

… and I love you

with no beginning and no end,

because you are my child

and I am your mama.

For my mother, whose love encircles us —G.S.

For Charlie —M.L.

PHILOMEL BOOKS
An imprint of Penguin Random House LLC, New York

First published in the United States of America by Philomel Books, an imprint of Penguin Random House LLC, 2021
Text copyright © 2021 by Gillian Sze • Illustrations copyright © 2021 by Michelle Lee

Philomel Books is a registered trademark of Penguin Random House LLC.

Visit us online at penguinrandomhouse.com. • Library of Congress Cataloging-in-Publication Data is available.

Manufactured in China • ISBN 9780593203071

1 3 5 7 9 10 8 6 4 2

Edited by Talia Benamy • Design by Monique Sterling • Text set in Horley Old Style • The illustrations were rendered in colored pencil and gouache.

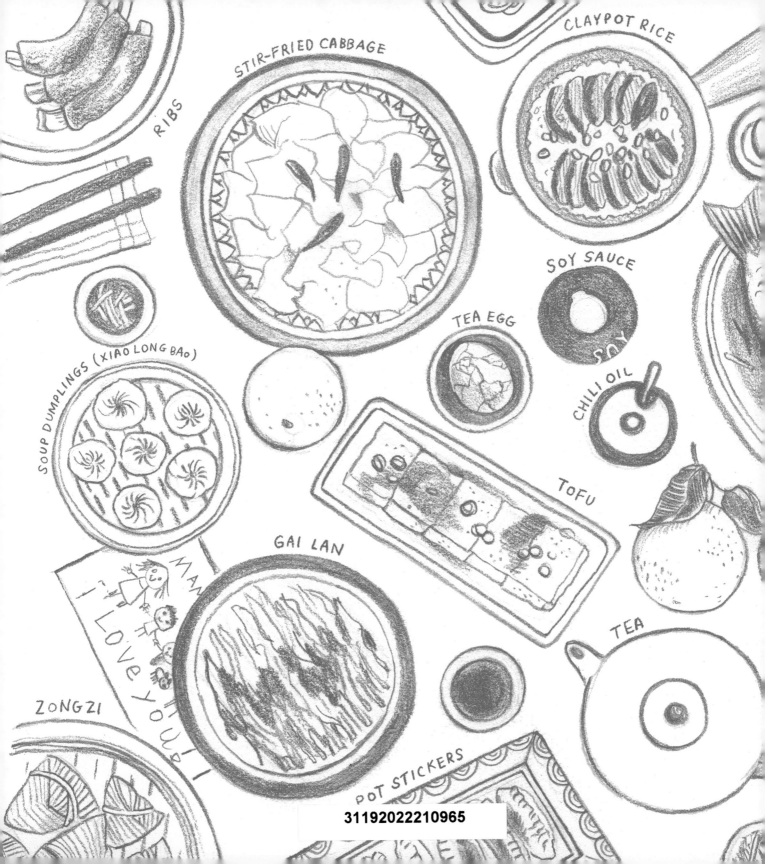